Sometimes

Algunas veces

Sometimes
Algunas veces

Keith Baker

Green Light Readers
Colección Luz Verde
Harcourt, Inc.

Orlando   Austin   New York
San Diego   Toronto   London

Sometimes I am happy.
Algunas veces estoy contento.

Sometimes I am sad.

Algunas veces estoy triste.

I like who I am.
Me gusta quien soy.

I like what I do.
Me gusta lo que hago.

Sometimes I am hot.
Algunas veces tengo calor.

Sometimes I am cold.

Algunas veces tengo frío.

I like who I am.

Me gusta quien soy.

I like what I do.
Me gusta lo que hago.

Sometimes I am up.

Algunas veces estoy arriba.

Sometimes I am down.

Algunas veces estoy abajo.

I like who I am.
Me gusta quien soy.

I like what I do.
Me gusta lo que hago.

Sometimes I am red.

Algunas veces me alegro.

Sometimes I am blue.

Algunas veces me entristezco.

I'm all of these things. What about you?
Soy todas estas cosas. ¿Y tú?

Do you sometimes wish to be different?
Who or what would you like to be?
Make a mask to show your family and friends!

Mask Yourself

1 Draw and cut out your mask.

2 Glue it to a paper plate.

3 Tape a Popsicle stick to the back.

- paper plate
- paper
- scissors
- glue
- crayons or markers
- Popsicle stick
- tape

Hold the mask in front of your face. Act like your mask!

¿Te gustaría algunas veces ser diferente?
¿Qué quisieras ser?
Haz una máscara y enséñasela a tus amigos
y familiares.

Ponte una máscara

1 Dibuja y recorta tu máscara.

2 Pégala a un plato de papel.

3 Pégale detrás una paleta de helado.

- plato de papel
- papel
- tijeras
- goma de pegar
- crayones o marcadores
- paleta de helado
- cinta adhesiva

Sujeta la máscara delante de tu cara. ¡Actúa como lo que representa tu máscara!

Meet the Author-Illustrator
Te presentamos al autor-ilustrador

Dear Boys and Girls,

My favorite color is green because I was born on St. Patrick's Day. When I was a boy, I loved to swim and ride my bike, just like the alligator in the story!

I still like to swim and ride my bike. I also like to work in my garden and cook. And, of course, I like to draw and paint. I really DO like what I do!

Queridos niños y niñas:

Mi color favorito es el verde, porque nací el día de San Patricio. De niño me gustaba nadar y montar en bicicleta, ¡como el cocodrilo del cuento!

Me sigue gustando nadar y montar en bicicleta. También me gusta cuidar mi jardín y cocinar. Y por supuesto, me gusta dibujar y pintar. Realmente, ¡ME ENCANTA lo que hago!

Keith Baker

www.HarcourtBooks.com

First Green Light Readers/Colección Luz Verde edition 2007

Green Light Readers is a trademark of Harcourt, Inc., registered in the
United States of America and/or other jurisdictions.

Library of Congress Cataloging-in-Publication Data
Baker, Keith, 1953–
[Sometimes. Spanish & English]
Sometimes = Algunas veces/Keith Baker.
p. cm.
"Green Light Readers."
Summary: An alligator feels different things from time to time, but they are all okay.
[1. Emotions—Fiction. 2. Senses and sensation—Fiction. 3. Self-acceptance—Fiction.
4. Alligators—Fiction. 5. Spanish language materials—Bilingual.] I. Title.
II. Title: Algunas veces. III. Series: Green Light Reader.
PZ73.B27155 2007
[E]—dc22   2006009514
ISBN 978-0-15-205959-0
ISBN 978-0-15-205961-3 (pb)

A C E G H F D B
C E G H F D (pb)

Ages 4–6
Grade: 1
Guided Reading Level: D
Reading Recovery Level: 6

Green Light Readers
For the reader who's ready to GO!

Five Tips to Help Your Child Become a Great Reader

1. Get involved. Reading aloud to and with your child is just as important as encouraging your child to read independently.

2. Be curious. Ask questions about what your child is reading.

3. Make reading fun. Allow your child to pick books on subjects that interest her or him.

4. Words are everywhere—not just in books. Practice reading signs, packages, and cereal boxes with your child.

5. Set a good example. Make sure your child sees YOU reading.

Why Green Light Readers Is the Best Series for Your New Reader

• Created exclusively for beginning readers by some of the biggest and brightest names in children's books

• Reinforces the reading skills your child is learning in school

• Encourages children to read—and finish—books by themselves

• Offers extra enrichment through fun, age-appropriate activities unique to each story

• Incorporates characteristics of the Reading Recovery program used by educators

• Developed with Harcourt School Publishers and credentialed educational consultants